the bears who stayed ˉˉˉˉ rs

susanna gretz · alison sage

A & C BLACK · LONDON

Once on a rainy day there were four bears in bed:
William, Charles, John, and Andrew.
Robert had already got up to bring the others
a cup of tea.
Under the bed was a dog, whose name was Fred.

In the bathroom, Charles read the newspaper.
"It says here that there's a rocket going
into space today," he said.
William was brushing his teeth.
He brushed his bottom teeth up
and his top teeth down.
"I'm hungry," he thought.
"It must be time for breakfast."

William ate grapefruit, bacon, scrambled eggs,
butter, toast and marmalade.
Charles ate hardly anything.
"Look at this," he said, reading the cereal packet.
"It tells you all about space rockets."
Andrew looked at the rain.
"What shall we do today?" he asked.
"We could go into space," said John.

"Let's wait until it stops raining,"
said Andrew.
"We can do the housework first."
Soon everyone was at work, dusting,
polishing, and making the beds.

But it went on raining and raining.
They opened the door and looked out.
There wasn't a bear in sight.
Robert put out one paw.
"It's too wet for a space flight," he said.
"We could go into space indoors."
"Indoors," agreed the others.

The chief scientist looked through his telescope.
He waited until the full moon was ready.
The flight commander checked his equipment.
William packed the food for the flight.

"Ready for take-off?" said the chief scientist.
"Ready," called Robert from down below.
"Blast off!" shouted the flight commander.
  He and the space dog took off slowly into space.

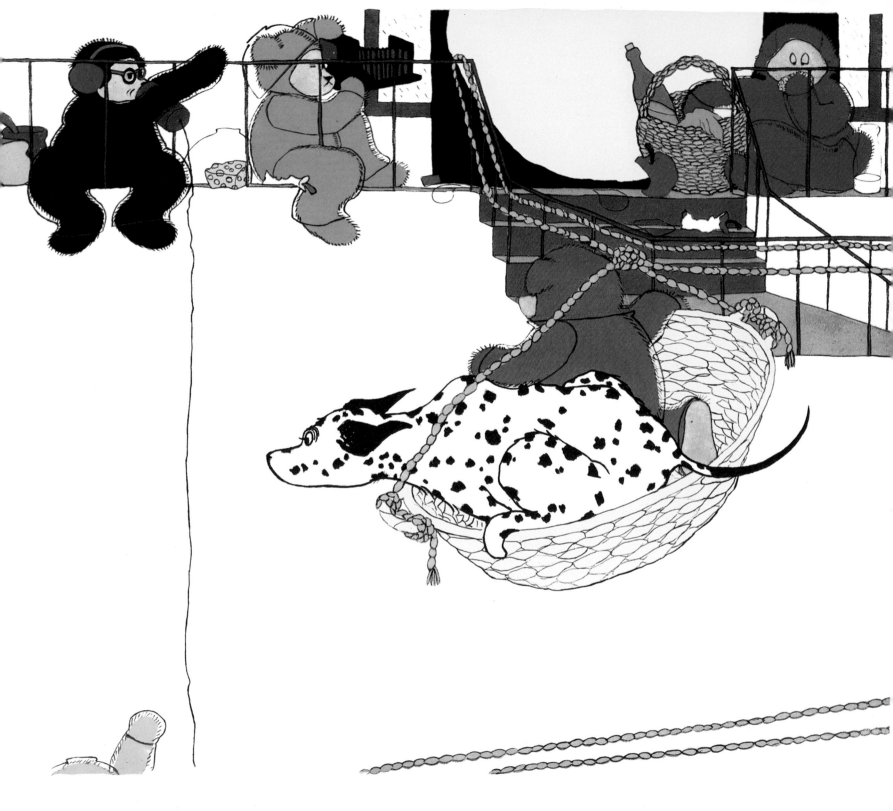

It was a perfect flight.
Everyone except Fred liked space travel.
Before long he jumped out of the spaceship.
"I've had enough, too," said Robert.
The ropes were getting tight around his middle.
Besides, he couldn't help noticing that
someone had eaten most of the space food.

Then everyone helped tidy up the spaceship.
John folded up the moon.
"I wonder where the real moon is," said Charles,
looking through his telescope.
"We'll have to take more food next time,"
said Robert.
"We could have some food now," said William.

They went into the kitchen
and Charles found a recipe for mooncakes.
"They'll take ten minutes to bake," he said.
John cut the cakes into moon shapes
and put them on the baking tray.
"William! Stop licking the spoon," he said.
"You'll be sick."

Soon the mooncakes were ready,
and Andrew passed them round.
"Don't I look like a waiter?" he said.
Robert waved his spoon in the air.
"I want jam on my cakes," he said.
"Look out!" said William.
"You're spilling it everywhere."

After supper, they cleared up the mess
in the kitchen.
"What a lot of dishes to wash," grumbled John.
"I'll help you in a minute," said William,
his mouth full of biscuits.
Fred stared at the tin of dog food.
He was waiting for someone to remember
his supper.

Later, John and Fred watched the space launch
while Charles read and the others played cards.
Even Fred was interested.
"I wonder if space travellers eat apples,"
said William.
"Hurry up!" said Robert.
"We've got to finish this game before bedtime."
But soon it *was* time for bed.

First they had a bath.
There was so much steam that John
drew a space dog on the mirror.
"What is steam?" asked Robert.
"Don't know," said Charles. "I'll
look it up tomorrow."
William was gargling with his
peppermint-flavoured mouthwash.
"It's funny," he thought.
"Gargling always makes me hungry."

The five bears hopped into bed.
William was already dreaming of breakfast.
"What about our exercises?" said Charles.
"Tomorrow," said John, drawing his
  bed picture.
"We could go to the jungle tomorrow," said Charles.
"It says here that the jungle is very interesting."
  But there was no answer.
  The other bears were fast asleep –
  and so was Fred.

This edition first published in paperback in 1999
by A & C Black (Publishers) Ltd.
35 Bedford Row
London WC1R 4JH

ISBN 0-7136-5226-8

First published in hardback in 1970
by Ernest Benn Limited
Reprinted 1972, 1974, 1981, 1983.
Second edition 1987. Reprinted 1993.

Illustration copyright © Susanna Gretz 1970
Text copyright © Alison Sage 1987